LULU
and the
HUNGER
MONSTER™

by Erik Talkin
illustrated by Sheryl Murray

free spirit
PUBLISHING®

Library of Congress Cataloging-in-Publication Data
Names: Talkin, Erik, author. | Murray, Sheryl, illustrator.
Title: Lulu and the hunger monster / by Erik Talkin ; illustrated by Sheryl Murray.
Description: Minneapolis, MN : Free Spirit Publishing Inc., [2020] | Audience: Ages 5–9. |
Identifiers: LCCN 2020008258 (print) | LCCN 2020008259 (ebook) | ISBN 9781631985461 (hardcover)
    | ISBN 9781631985478 (pdf) | ISBN 9781631985485 (epub)
Subjects: CYAC: Hunger—Fiction. | Secrets—Fiction. | Schools—Fiction. | Friendship—Fiction.
Classification: LCC PZ7.1.T348 Lul 2020 (print) | LCC PZ7.1.T348 (ebook) | DDC [E]—dc23
LC record available at https://lccn.loc.gov/2020008258
LC ebook record available at https://lccn.loc.gov/2020008259

Free Spirit Publishing does not have control over or assume responsibility for author or third-party websites and their content.

Reading Level Grade 2; Interest Level Ages 5–9
Fountas & Pinnell Guided Reading Level M

Edited by Alison Behnke
Cover and interior design by Emily Dyer

10 9 8 7 6 5 4 3
Printed in China
R18861221

Free Spirit Publishing Inc.
6325 Sandburg Road, Suite 100
Minneapolis, MN 55427-3674
(612) 338-2068
help4kids@freespirit.com
freespirit.com

FSC
www.fsc.org
MIX
Paper from
responsible sources
FSC® C144853

For Mari (without whom . . .);
Ella, Felix, Lili, Hannah, Max, & Mia;
and a hunger-free future that starts today.
—E.T.

For Dad:
Thank you for a lifetime of love and support.
Always remember—the Driver is the Chief Guru.
—S.M.

With a **GRIND** and a **CLANK,** our old van slows to a stop. Mom can't start it.

Monster waves from the roadside. "Hi, Lulu. Long time no see."

When we get a ride home, Monster buckles in next to me.

All Mom's money goes to fix the van.
She needs it to drive to work. That means
there's no money left for groceries.

Mom says she doesn't think
we can get help because
she has a job.

So we make do.
And make do.

Ava runs up to me at school, her half of our twin necklaces dancing.
She can't see Monster **SMIRKING**. And I can't tell her.

Monster made me promise never
to say its name to anyone:
HUNGER MONSTER.

"Tell me one of your jokes," Ava says.

All I can think about is food, food, food.

"Why do the French eat snails?" I ask.
"Because they don't like fast food."

Ava laughs and we join our friends to play tag before the bell. Soon I have to sit.

My head is **SPINNING**.
My stomach is **NOISY**.

Hunger Monster
is **GROWLING**.

In math, Monster bounces on my table so the numbers **SQUIGGLE** and **JIGGLE**.
Mr. Abidi turns around. "Lulu, please sit still."

I want to tell him it's Hunger Monster's fault. Monster **GLARES** at me.
So my mouth stays closed.

During morning recess, Ava wants to play.
My stomach is empty and achy, and I yell at her.
She doesn't know why I'm being so grumpy.

I go hide in the school garden.

This year, Mr. Abidi is teaching us how to plant vegetables.
Maybe there's something to eat in here. But the tomatoes
are still green and hard. I kick at them.

"Temper, temper," Hunger Monster says. "You know what you are? *Hangry*. Hungry *and* angry. I invented that!" Hunger Monster beams.

The bell rings and I leave Monster gloating in the weeds.

I always get free school lunch, so Monster will hide this afternoon.
SULKING in the hallways.
WAITING for another chance.

Hunger Monster bugs me the most before lunch, in the morning.
Mornings like this one.

I can't stop thinking about the cubbies out in the hallway, stuffed full
of everyone's snacks. "Can I go to the restroom, please?"

In the hall I reach for someone's lunchbox.

Ants on a Log—my **FAVORITE**.
I stare for a long time.

Then I turn away.
Hunger Monster won't make me a thief.

Monster waddles off in a HUFF.
And I make do.

Next morning, Ava passes me a bag. "I've got too much snack."
Inside are grapes, yogurt, and cauliflower.

I don't want to take it. My face feels hot.
I only take the bag because Ava is my friend.

Monster shrinks that day.
And the next, when Veronica
has too much fruit salad.

And the next, when
Manuel wants help
with a spare tamale.

By Friday, Hunger Monster's no bigger than a toy.

"Everyone's whispering and laughing about you," it squeaks.
After that, I don't take any more snacks—
not even from Ava.

A few days later, Mom gives me a bag for snack time. **"SURPRISE!"**
There's a sunbutter sandwich and string cheese.

I peek inside her lunch bag. Plain crackers and packets of ketchup.
"Looks like I should spend today with your mom," Monster says.

"No! I won't let you!" I slip my string cheese into Mom's bag.

"That's cheating!" Monster says. "No matter. It will be gone soon, and I'll be back."

My shoulders slump. I can't keep standing up to this monster all by myself.

At recess, I decide to talk to Mr. Abidi. Even though my stomach is full of snacks today, it still **ACHES** as I go to find him.

I've never said Hunger Monster's name out loud.
Even so, I have to do something.

For Mom.
And for me.

Mr. Abidi is tying up the tomato plants and taking out the broken stakes.
The ones I broke.

As I unlatch the gate to the garden, Monster **LOOMS** over me.
"He'll think your mom is a bad person."

I almost walk away.
But I can't let Hunger Monster trick me again.

Ava comes up behind me and takes my hand.

"Lulu, today I have a joke for you. Why shouldn't you tell jokes to eggs? They might crack up."

I want to smile, but I can't. "I have to go talk to Mr. Abidi."

Ava nods. "Let me come with you."

Together, we pull weeds as I talk to Mr. Abidi.

About the car trouble.
About how Mom's getting paid soon.
But not soon enough.

Mr. Abidi says he's glad I talked to him. "I know about a place that can help."

Now my tummy feels fine.

Mom and I visit a food pantry. A truck from the food bank drops off healthy food.

Everything's free, and we pick what we need.

Everyone helps each other. Except Monster.

Mom and I head
home in our van, leaving
Hunger Monster far behind—for today.

Tonight, we're cooking a yummy meal
together. I'm excited to help.

And next week, I'm going to help at the food pantry.

Because Hunger Monster is strong.
But so are we.

You Can Stand Up to the Hunger Monster

Lulu's story is that of many kids and many families. In my own community, I have helped families like hers through my work at the Foodbank of Santa Barbara County. A food bank is a big warehouse that stores food and provides it free of cost to people who are hungry. The organization Feeding America has food banks all over the country that store and supply fresh and healthy food for tens of thousands of local food pantries and programs. Other organizations, such as Share Our Strength and Bread for the World, are also part of the fight against the Hunger Monster.

According to Feeding America, one in seven children in the United States lives with hunger. After families pay bills or deal with emergencies—like Lulu's broken-down van—they don't always have enough money left for healthy food. People can feel too awkward, embarrassed, or ashamed to ask for help. And so the Hunger Monster can stay invisible.

Your family might face hunger sometimes. You probably go to school with kids who don't always have enough to eat at home—even if you don't know it. And in your community, there are always people who need help.

What can you do to help? Whether it's you, someone you know, or a stranger facing hunger, you *can* stand up to the Hunger Monster—and you don't have to do it alone.

- The first thing to do is remember that this is a tough issue, and that you can help by simply being sensitive and caring toward people who you think might need more food. For example, rather than waiting for someone to ask for help, you could offer to share food with someone who might not have enough so they don't feel awkward about accepting it.

- You could help plan, organize, or run a food drive at your school to collect canned goods and other food.

- You and a friend or family member could volunteer at a food pantry.

- You could talk to your teacher about starting a school garden.

- If you realize that someone might not always be getting enough food, invite them over to play. Then you can ask them to stay for lunch or dinner without making a big deal about it.

- If you bring a snack, take some extra food to share with a friend.

- Like Ava in the story, you could support a friend just by listening and caring.

- You could ask a teacher, a counselor, a coach, or another adult you trust for help. The Hunger Monster wants everyone to keep quiet, but you can refuse to play the Monster's game.

These are just some of the ways that you can help others, or yourself. Together, we can chase away the Hunger Monster.

For good.

For more information on how to stand up to the Hunger Monster, visit **freespirit.com/leader** to download a free leader's guide with additional information, discussion questions, and activity ideas you can use in your classroom and community.

About the Author and Illustrator

Erik Talkin, CEO of the Foodbank of Santa Barbara County, is a recognized innovator and leader in America's food bank network. Previously, he was a Board Member of the California Association of Food Banks and sat on the National Advisory Council of Feeding America. Committed to helping people move from simple charity to building long-term food security, Erik has authored *Hunger into Health* and has helped create innovative and national award-winning children's nutrition education programs such as Healthy School Pantry and Kid's Farmers Market.

Erik is also a writer and filmmaker and has served as a principal in two production companies. His short film *The Gallery*, starring Helena Bonham Carter, was selected for the London Film Festival. He has won an International Television Association Award for writing and directing educational drama and his theatrical work has been produced on the London Fringe. Erik lives in Santa Barbara, California. Visit his website at eriktalkin.com.

Sheryl Murray grew up in a big family of eight kids where storytelling happened every day, whether it was putting on shows in the backyard, making up bedtime stories or convincing her mom that it couldn't possibly have been her who drew on the baby. She now lives in Portland, Oregon, where she illustrates books for kids, makes up funny voices for her cats, and occasionally banishes a tricky monster of her own with the help of her two brave girls. Learn more about Sheryl and her work at sherylmurray.com/portfolio.

Other Great Books from Free Spirit

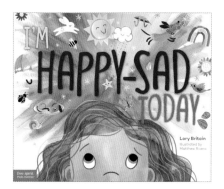

I'm Happy-Sad Today
Making Sense of Mixed-Together Feelings
by Lory Britain, Ph.D., illustrated by Matthew Rivera
For ages 3–8. 40 pp.; HC; full-color; 11¼" x 9¼".

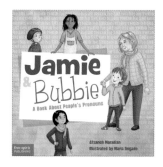

Jamie and Bubbie
A Book About People's Pronouns
by Afsaneh Moradian,
illustrated by Maria Bogade
For ages 4–8. 32 pp.; HC; full-color;
8" x 8".

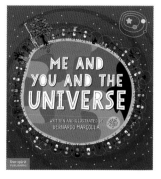

Me and You and the Universe
written and illustrated by Bernardo Marçolla
For ages 3–8. 36 pp.; HC w/ jacket; full-color;
8¼" x 9".

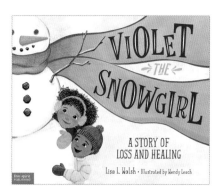

Violet the Snowgirl
A Story of Loss and Healing
by Lisa L. Walsh, illustrated by Wendy Leach
For ages 5–10. 40 pp.; HC; full-color; 11¼" x 9¼".

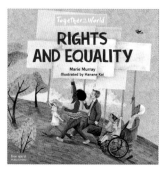

Rights and Equality
by Marie Murray, illustrated by Hanane Kai
For ages 6–10. 32 pp.; HC; full-color;
8½" x 8½".

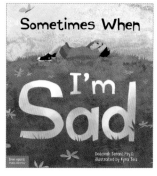

Sometimes When I'm Sad
by Deborah Serani, Psy.D., illustrated by Kyra Teis
For ages 4-8. 40 pp.; HC; full-color; 8¼" x 9".

Interested in purchasing multiple quantities and receiving volume discounts?
Contact edsales@freespirit.com or call 1.800.735.7323 and ask for Education Sales.

Many Free Spirit authors are available for speaking engagements, workshops, and keynotes.
Contact speakers@freespirit.com or call 1.800.735.7323.

For pricing information, to place an order, or to request a free catalog, contact:

Free Spirit Publishing Inc. • 6325 Sandburg Road • Suite 100 • Minneapolis, MN 55427-3674
toll-free 800.735.7323 • local 612.338.2068 • fax 612.337.5050 • help4kids@freespirit.com • freespirit.com